Puddle

By Richard Jackson

Illustrated by Chris Raschka

GREENWILLOW BOOKS
AN IMPRINT OF HARPERCOLLINSPUBLISHERS

For our dear Cazets, with love:
Donna, Denys, Scott,
Alex, and Jack—R. J.

To Dick—C. R.

Puddle
Text copyright © 2019 by Richard Jackson.
Illustrations copyright © 2019 by Chris Raschka.
All rights reserved. Manufactured in China.
For information address HarperCollins Children's Books,
a division of HarperCollins Publishers, 195 Broadway,
New York, NY 10007. www.harpercollinschildrens.com
Watercolor and gouache paint on paper were used
to prepare the full-color art. The text type is ITC Avant
Garde Gothic.

Library of Congress Cataloging-in-Publication Data
Names: Jackson, Richard, author. |
   Raschka, Christopher, illustrator.
Title: Puddle / by Richard Jackson; illustrated by
   Chris Raschka.
Description: First edition. | New York, NY: Greenwillow
   Books, an imprint of HarperCollins Publishers, (2019) |
Summary: A puddle sits despairingly as she is
   trampled on by humans and animals alike until
   something miraculous happens that makes her
   feel worthwhile.
Identifiers: LCCN 2018003455 | ISBN 9780062651952
   (hardcover)
Subjects: | CYAC: Puddles—Fiction. | Self-acceptance—
   Fiction.
Classification: LCC PZ7.1.J35 Pu 2019 | DDC (E)—dc23 LC
   record available at https://lccn.loc.gov/2018003455

19 20 21 22 23 SCP 10 9 8 7 6 5 4 3 2 1
First Edition
Greenwillow Books

rain

rain

RAIN

RAIN

"Enough," Puddle mutters.

"I mean, look at me,
a sight to see—
        Puddle the Pudge.
And look at the *others*,
    my sisters and brothers,
so dainty and sweet,
        so shallow . . .

"Oh, I don't know. . . .
It's no fun
being the deep one.
If this rain keeps on,
I'll soon be a POND.
I'll soon . . ."

Swoosh!

A seagull swoops in.

"Nice! Smells of fish . . ."

Swish!

Puddle looks up.

"Yikes! A basketball!"
Gull goes.
"Recess already, I suppose."
Her brothers and sisters . . . do they care?
Not a whit.
The rain, a drizzle now,
dimples them bit by bit. . . .

Splat!

A sneaker
with a hole in the toe—
two toes
showing.

Euwww.

"I wish I had a drain," she moans,
and imagines the flowing,
gurgling
whirlpool
she could make of herself—
the *Ahhh-ing* and *Ohhh-ing*.

Splash!

Four paws.

Uh-oh.

Smells like . . .

wet poodle.

"No piddle," Puddle cries.

"No, **NO!**"

Too late . . .
"Oh, that's just swell!"
Did they see,
all the others?

Across the playground
the sisters, the brothers, are
one by one
dimming
like night-lights at dawn,
winking out . . .
drying up
in sudden sunshine—

Puddle is alone.

Finally . . .

A bell rings. *Brrring*

feet (repeat)

feet

FEET

FEET!

"Hold it!" Puddle shouts,

but who has heard?

Still, the children halt. Hands point.

Puddle looks, too—overhead,

then at herself.

"Oh, my word!"

Puddle blushes

red

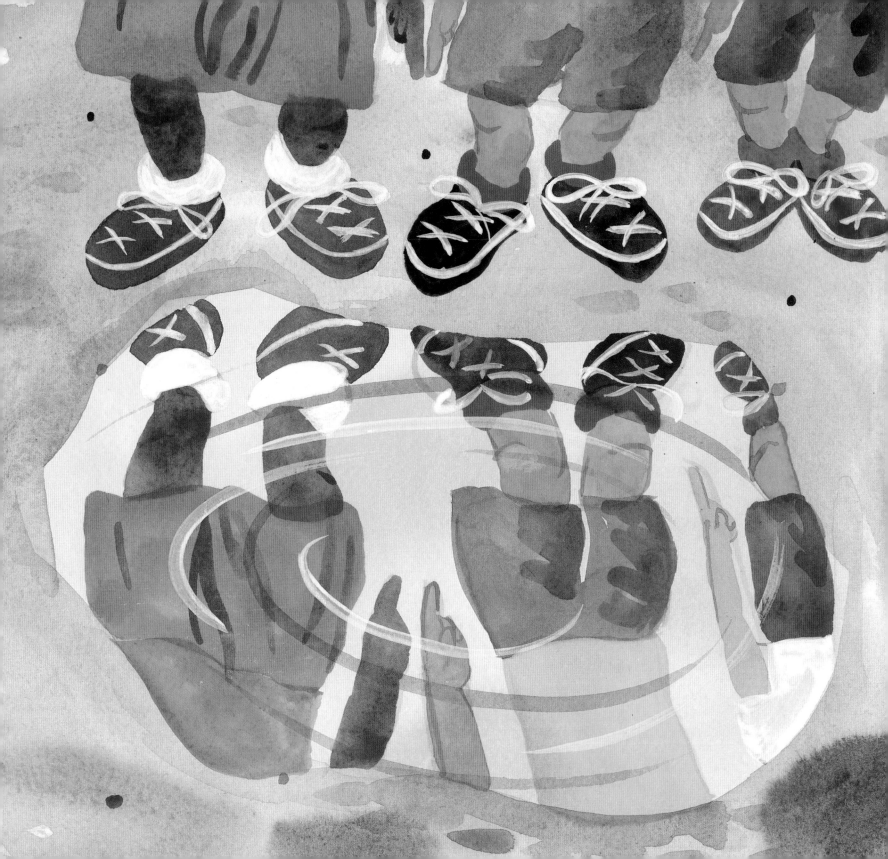

orange

yellow

green

blue

violet

echoing the sky.

Applause, applause!

A chorus of *Ohhhs* and *Ahhhs*.

She is, indeed, a sight to see

is our Puddle.

A small girl
in Mary Janes
          remains.
She reaches out
to Puddle.
     "Look," the girl says,
and sees the colors
          shiver and shimmer,
          one by one.

The gull,
the shoe,
the dog,
the ball?
Puddle forgets them
each by each. . . .

But the reach—
that is everything!

That is all.